THE ADVENTURES OF
TOM SAWYER

THE ADVENTURES OF
TOM SAWYER

by
Mark Twain

Abridged, adapted,
and illustrated
by
quadrum■

Modern Publishing
A Division of Kappa Books Publishers, LLC.

Cover art by Quadrum

Contents

CHAPTER 1

Whitewashing the Fence

"Tom!"

There was no answer.

"What's wrong with him, I wonder?"

The old lady looked around the room but could not see the boy anywhere. "Well, if I get hold of you, I'll—"

She bent down and poked under the bed with her long broom. She was out of breath. Only the cat, who ran out from underneath, answered with a loud yowl.

The old lady walked over to the open door and looked out at the garden; she yelled again, "Y-o-u-u, Tom!"

She heard a little noise behind her and turned around just in time to grab a small boy by the baggy seat of his dun-

9

garees. "There! What were you doing in there?"

"Nothing."

"Nothing! Look at your hands, and mouth—what is that?"

"I don't know, Aunt."

"Well, I know. It's jam. I keep telling you not to touch that jam!" She raised her hand to hit him . . .

"Look behind you, Aunt!"

The old lady whirled around and snatched her skirts out of danger. The boy scrambled up the high board fence and disappeared over it.

Aunt Polly stood there surprised for a moment, and then laughed gently.

"Oh! I never learn! He's played that trick on me so many times. He knows how to hassle me and then he makes me laugh! My own dead sister's boy, poor thing, and I don't have the heart to whack him, even if he is really bad. But tomorrow he will have to do some work for me—it's the only way to punish him. I have to see that he is a good boy. It's my duty!"

Tom's younger half brother Sidney had already finished his part of the work of picking up wood chips. Sid was a quiet boy and had no adventurous, troublesome ways.

During supper, Aunt Polly asked Tom questions to find out what he did in the afternoon. "It was warm in school, wasn't it? Didn't you swim, Tom?"

Tom replied, "Not very much."

"But you aren't too warm now."

She was pleased to know that the shirt was dry without anyone knowing what she wanted to know. But Tom was a clever boy and he knew. "Some of us pumped water on our heads—mine's damp still. See?"

"Tom, you didn't have to undo your shirt collar where I sewed it to pump on your head. Unbutton your jacket!"

Tom opened his jacket. His shirt collar was still tightly sewed.

But Sid had seen something.

"I thought you sewed his collar with white thread, but it's black," said Sid.

"I did sew it with white thread! Tom!"

Tom ran out the door.

In a few minutes, he had forgotten everything. He had found something new to figure out—a new whistle. It was a funny bird-like sound, made by touching the tongue to the roof of the mouth at short intervals. He soon managed to do it and walked down the street whistling happily.

The summer evenings were long. A little way down the street Tom stopped whistling and looked at someone in front of him. He was a stranger—a boy just a shade larger than he was—well dressed with a nice cap, new blue cloth dungarees, and polished shoes. He even wore a necktie and a bright ribbon. He was a city boy.

The boys looked at each other, all around. Then Tom said, "I can lick you!"

"I'd like to see you try it."

Tom said, "What's your name?"

"None of your business."

They argued a bit and slowly moved

closer and closer together.

Soon they were rolling in the dirt, tugging and tearing, punching and scratching, covered with dust. The fight slowed down, the dust settled, and Tom was seen sitting on top of the new boy, pounding him with his fists.

The boy struggled to get free. At last, he said, "Enough!"

Then Tom said, "Better look out who you're fooling with next time."

The new boy ran off, brushing the dust from his clothes, sobbing, looking back now and again and shaking his head and threatening what he would do to Tom the "next time we meet." Tom jeered back and started walking away. But the boy threw a stone that hit Tom on the back. Then Tom ran behind the boy and found out his house. He waited at the gate yelling for the new boy to dare come out. But the boy's mother looked out and called Tom a bad child and told him to go away. Tom went, but he said he would "show" him!

Tom got home pretty late. When he climbed in the window, he bumped right into his aunt. She told him that Saturday would not be a holiday for him. "And no arguing with me, young man!"

Saturday morning arrived and Tom appeared on the sidewalk with a bucket of whitewash and a long-handled brush. He looked at the fence—thirty yards of board slats, each nine feet high. This was not going to be easy. He dipped his brush in the paint and began. One stroke was enough for him. He sat down on a tree stump and began to think. Soon his friends would come by on all sorts of wonderful expeditions and they would make fun of him. There was nothing in his pockets he could give them to make them take over. He thought hard. And had a great big fabulous idea. He took up his brush and went happily to work.

Ben Rogers walked up to him, eating an apple.

Ben stared and then said, "Hi! You're in a bit of a mess, ain't you!"

Tom didn't answer, but looked at his work carefully. His mouth watered for the apple, but he stuck to his work.

Ben said, "You gotta work, hey?"

Tom said, "What do you call work?"

"Why, ain't that work?"

Tom returned to his work and replied,
"Well, all I know is, it suits Tom."

"Oh, do you mean that you like it?"

"I don't see why I shouldn't."

Ben stopped nibbling his apple. Tom swept his brush back and forth and stepped back to see how it looked.

Ben watched him and then said, "Tom, let me whitewash a little."

"No, Ben!"

"Lemme try. I'll give you my apple."

Tom gave Ben the brush. While Ben worked and sweated in the sun, Tom sat down and munched his apple. Then many boys came by and stayed on to paint. By afternoon, Tom had collected a lot of stuff, including a brass doorknob.

CHAPTER 2

Tom Meets Becky

Tom stood in front of Aunt Polly by an open window of the bedroom.

Tom said, "May I go and play now?"

"How much have you done?"

"It's all done, Aunt."

She didn't believe him. She went to see for herself. She was surprised when she found the fence nicely whitewashed. "Oh, great! Go and play, Tom. But come home soon."

She was so pleased with him that she gave him a nice apple. While she was talking, Tom took a doughnut and hid it in his pocket. Then he ran out of the

19

house.

Tom hopped and skipped toward the public square of the village. As he was passing the house where Lawyer Jeff Thatcher lived, he saw a new girl in the garden—a lovely little blue-eyed girl with yellow hair in braids, wearing a white summer frock. Tom looked at her and fell instantly in love. He stared at her and began to show off. Suddenly, he saw that she was walking back to

her house and he sighed, very loudly. But now, she knew he was watching and she threw him a flower.

Tom picked it up with his toes and, in an instant, shoved it into his jacket. He did a few more acrobatics, but she never came out again, so, finally, Tom went home.

He thought about the girl all the time.

The next morning, it was time to dress for Sunday School. Sidney's older sister, Mary, washed and scrubbed him. She combed him and helped him wear his clothes, making sure that everything was set right.

Tom looked very nice. His shoes were nicely polished. But he was uncomfortable.

Soon Mary was ready, too. She, Sid and Tom set out for Sunday School.

Sunday School hours were from nine to half past ten; and then church service.

Tom's whole class was noisy and troublesome. When they came to recite their lessons, not one of them knew his verses, but had to be prompted. And when they were done, each got his reward, in small blue tickets, each with a passage of the Scripture on it; each blue ticket was pay for two verses of recitation. Ten blue tickets equalled a red one; ten red tickets equalled a yellow one; for ten yellow tickets the superintendent gave a Bible to the pupil.

Then Mr. Walters, the Sunday School teacher, commanded everybody's attention. "Now, children, I want you all to sit straight and give me all your attention for a minute or two."

Suddenly, a middle-aged gentleman with iron-gray hair, and a dignified lady came into the church. The lady was holding the hand of a young girl, and Tom's heart leaped.

Mr. Walters introduced the visitors to the school. The middle-aged man was the county judge from Constantinople, twelve miles away. This was the great Judge Thatcher, brother of Jeff Thatcher.

There was only one thing that could make Mr. Walters really happy—a chance to present a Bible prize. But no one had enough tickets to get

one except Tom. He wanted a Bible. Walters was not expecting this at all. But it was happening. So Tom got to sit with the judge and his family. Tom was introduced to the judge; the judge put his hand on Tom's head and asked him what his name was. Tom stammered, "Thomas Sawyer, sir."

"That's a good boy! Now, I am sure you know the names of all the twelve disciples. Who were the first two?"

Tom blushed.

"I know you'll tell me," said the lady. "The names of the first two disciples were—"

"DAVID AND GOLIATH!"

CHAPTER 3

The Loose Tooth

About half past ten, Sunday School ended and the church bell began to ring. People gathered for the morning sermon. The Sunday School children sat with their parents. Tom, Sid, and Mary sat with Aunt Polly. Tom sat there, bored.

Then he remembered a large black beetle, a pinchbug, he called it, that he had in his pocket in a small box. He opened the box and the beetle climbed out. It bit Tom. Tom flung it away. The beetle went floundering into the aisle and lay on its back, out of reach, and the hurt finger went into Tom's mouth. Other people watched the beetle. A poodle came along.

25

He saw the beetle; his drooping tail lifted and wagged. He looked at the bug, walked around it, sniffed at it from a safe distance, took a closer smell, and tried to bite it. The beetle bit him back, and the poodle yelped and tossed his head. The beetle fell a couple of yards away, on its back once more. Tom was happy. The dog looked foolish, but wanted revenge. So he went to the beetle and began a wary attack on it again; jumping at it, making even closer snatches at it with

his teeth and jerking his head till his ears flapped. But he grew tired; he yawned, sighed, forgot the beetle entirely, and sat down on it. Then there was a wild yelp of agony and the poodle went running up the aisle; in front of the altar, down the other aisle, out of the window.

By this time the whole church was red-faced with suppressed laughter, and the sermon had come to a standstill. When it started again, people were giggling, trying not to laugh out loud. It was a relief when the minister said his final amen.

Tom went home, thinking that there was some satisfaction about divine service when there was a bit of variety in it.

The following day was Monday and Tom was miserable. Another week suffering in school. He wished he was sick; then he could stay home from school. But there was nothing wrong with him. Suddenly he discovered something. One of his upper front teeth was loose. Then it occurred to him that if his aunt noticed, she would pull it out, and that would hurt. So he thought he would look for something else for now. Tom drew his sore toe from under the sheet. It seemed worthwhile to chance it, so he groaned loudly.

Sid slept on. Tom groaned louder. Sid did not move. Tom began to groan again.

Sid yawned, stretched, then sat up and stared at Tom. Tom went on groaning.

Sid said, "What is the matter, Tom?"

Tom moaned, "Oh, don't bother me."

"I must call Aunt Polly."

"No, don't call anybody."

Sid ran out. Tom's imagination was working well, and his groans sounded real.

Sid ran downstairs. "Aunt Polly, come! Tom's dying!"

"Dying!" exclaimed Aunt Polly.

She ran upstairs with Sid and Mary. Her face was white, and her lip trembled.

"Tom! What's the matter with you?"

"Oh, Aunt Polly, my sore toe's dying!"

The old lady sat down and laughed a little, then cried a little. "Tom, shut up that nonsense and get up."

The groans stopped and the pain vanished from the toe. "Aunt Polly, it hurt, so I never minded my tooth at all."

"What's the matter with your tooth?"

"One of them's loose, and it aches."

"There now! Open your mouth."

Tom said, "Oh please, Auntie, don't pull it out. It don't hurt any more. I don't want to stay home from school."

"Oh, so all this was because you thought you'd get to stay home from school and go fishing? Tom, I love you so much, and you try every way you can to break my heart."

The old lady tied one end of a silk thread with a loop to Tom's tooth and tied the other to the bedpost. Then she grabbed a piece of hot coal and suddenly waved it in front of Tom's face. The tooth came out.

Tom was happy. He was the envy of every boy he met because the gap in his upper row of teeth allowed him to spit in a new way.

Soon Tom met Huckleberry Finn, son of the town drunkard. Huckleberry Finn was idle and lawless and vulgar and bad—and all the children admired him, liked being with him, and wanted to be

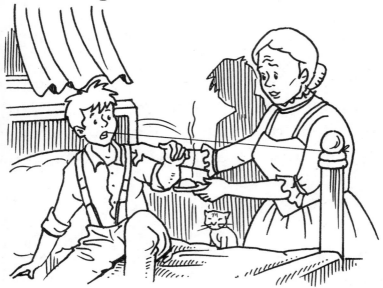

like him. Tom did, too.

Huckleberry Finn was always dressed in the cast-off clothes of grown-ups, which were torn and dirty. His hat was torn, too; his coat, when he wore one, hung nearly to his heels. One suspender held up his trousers, the seat bagged low, and the fringed legs dragged in the dirt if they were not rolled up.

Huckleberry Finn came and went at his own free will. He slept on doorsteps in fine weather and in empty barrels when it rained. He did not have to go to school or to church. He could go fishing or swimming when and where he chose, and stay as long as it suited him. Nobody told him not to fight; he could stay up as late as he pleased. He never had to wash, or put on clean clothes; he could swear wonderfully.

Tom yelled, "Hello, Huckleberry!"

"Hello yourself."

"What's that?"

"Dead cat."

"Say—what are dead cats good for?"

"Good for? Cure warts with."

"How do you cure the warts with the dead cats?"

"You take your cat and go in the graveyard and when it's midnight, a devil will come, but you can't see 'em, you can only hear something like the wind, or hear 'em talk; then you heave your cat after 'em and say, 'Devil follow corpse, cat follow devil, warts follow cat, I'm done with ye!' That'll fetch any wart."

"When you going to try the cat?"

"Tonight."

When Tom reached the schoolhouse, he strode in briskly. He hung his hat on a peg and flung himself into his seat. The master was dozing. The interruption roused him.

"Thomas Sawyer!"

Tom knew that when his name was pronounced in full, it meant trouble.

"Sir!"

"Come up here. Why are you late again, as usual?"

Tom was about to lie, when he saw two long tails of yellow hair hanging down a back that he recognized. There was the only vacant place on the girls' side of the schoolhouse.

He instantly said, "I stopped to talk with Huckleberry Finn!"

The master's stared and said, "What?"

"Stopped to talk with him."

"Thomas, take off your jacket."

The master whacked Tom until his arm was tired. "Now go and sit with the girls! And let this be a warning to you."

Tom sat down on the end of the pine bench, and the girl moved away from him with a toss of her head. He began to peek at the girl. She made a face at him and looked away. When she turned around again, a peach lay in front of her. She pushed it away. Tom scrawled on his slate, "Please take it—I got more." The girl looked, but made no sign. The boy began to draw something on the slate. For a while the girl refused to notice, but was curious. At last she peeked and said, "Let me see."

Tom uncovered a drawing of a house with two gable ends and a corkscrew of smoke coming from the chimney. The girl looked, then said, "It's nice, make a

man."

Then the artist drew a man.

"It's a beautiful man—now make me coming along."

Tom drew an hourglass with a full moon and straw limbs holding a fan.

The girl said, "It's so nice. I wish I could draw."

"It's easy," said Tom. "I'll teach you."

"Oh, will you? When?"

"At noon."

"Good—What's your name?"

"Becky Thatcher. What's yours? Oh, I know. It's Thomas Sawyer."

"You call me Tom, will you?"

"Yes."

Now Tom began to scrawl something on the slate, hiding the words from the girl. She begged to see. Tom said, "Oh, it ain't anything."

"Yes it is."

"You won't tell anybody at all?"

"No, I won't ever tell anybody."

She put her small hand on his, and Tom let his hand slip till these words were revealed: "I LOVE YOU."

"Oh, you bad thing!" And she hit his hand a smart rap, and blushed away.

CHAPTER 4

Tom's Heart Breaks

The harder Tom tried to concentrate, the more his mind wandered. So at last, he gave up. Tom wanted to do something of interest to pass the time. His hand wandered into his pocket and his face lit up—there was something! Then the small box slowly emerged. He released a tick that Huck had given to him and put him on the long flat desk. The creature started to travel off, but Tom turned him with a pin and made him take a new direction.

Tom's best friend, Joe Harper, sat next to him. The two boys were sworn friends all week, and enemies on

Saturdays. Joe took a pin out of his lapel and began to help play with the bug. Soon Tom said that they were interfering with each other, and neither was getting all the fun the tick could provide.

"Now," said Tom, "as long as he is on your side, you can stir him up and I'll let him alone; but if you let him get away to my side, I'll leave him alone as long as I can keep him from crossing over."

The tick escaped from Tom and crossed the equator. Joe harassed him awhile, and then he got away and crossed back again. The tick tried this, that, and the other, and got as excited as the boys did. But Joe kept him on his side. At last Tom could stand it no longer. So he reached out and lent a hand with his pin. Joe was angry. "Tom, you leave him alone."

"I want to stir him up a little, Joe."

"He's on my side of the line."

"Look here, Joe, whose tick is that?"

"I don't care whose tick he is—he's on my side of the line."

Suddenly, a tremendous whack came down on Tom's shoulders, and another on Joe's. The boys had not noticed the quiet before the master came tiptoeing down and stood over them. He had watched for a while and then waded in.

At noon, Tom flew to Becky. The two

met at the bottom of the lane, and when they reached the school they were all alone.

"Becky, was you ever engaged?"

"What's that?"

"Why, engaged to be married."

"No."

"Would you like to?"

"I reckon so. What is it like?"

"Like? You just tell a boy you won't ever have anybody but him, and then you kiss and that's all. Anybody can do it."

"Kiss? What do you kiss for?"

"Why, everybody that's in love with each other do that. Do you remember what I wrote on the slate?"

"Ye-yes."

"What was it?"

"I sha'n't tell you."

"Shall I tell you?"

"Ye-yes—but some other time."

"No, now."

"No, not now—tomorrow."

"Oh no, now. Becky, I'll whisper it."

Becky hesitating, Tom passed his arm about her waist and whispered in her ear, "Now you whisper it to me."

She resisted for a while, then said, "You turn your face, and then I will. But you mustn't ever tell anybody, will you, Tom?"

"No, indeed, I won't. Now, Becky."

He turned his face away. She bent timidly around till her breath stirred his curls, and whispered, "I—love—you!"

Then she sprang away and ran around the desks and benches, with Tom after her. Tom hugged her and said, "Now, Becky, it's all done—all over but the kiss. Don't you be afraid of that—please, Becky."

She gave up, and let her hands drop; her face came up. Tom kissed the red lips and said, "Now it's all done, Becky.

And always after this, you know, you ain't ever to love anybody but me, and you ain't ever to marry anybody but me. Will you?"

"No, I'll never love anybody but you, Tom, and I'll never marry anybody but you—and you ain't to ever marry anybody but me, either."

"Oh, yes! And always coming to school or when we're going home, you're to walk with me, when there ain't anybody looking, and we choose each other at parties."

"It's so nice."

"Yes, it is! Me and Amy Lawrence—"

The big eyes told Tom about his mistake and he stopped, confused.

"Oh, Tom! Then I ain't the first you've ever been engaged to!"

She began to cry. Tom said, "Oh, don't cry, Becky, I don't care for her anymore."

"Yes, you do, Tom, you know you do."

Tom tried to put his arm around her, but she pushed him away and went on crying. Tom tried again, but was pushed away.

"Becky," said Tom. "I-I don't care for anybody but you."

No reply—but sobs.

"Becky, won't you say something?"

Tom offered her his most precious treasure, a brass knob, and said, "Please, Becky, won't you take it?

She slapped his hand and the knob fell down. Tom marched out of the house and over the hills and far away. Becky ran to the door; he was not in sight. She flew around to the play yard; he was not there.

Then she called, "Tom! Come back."

There was no answer. So she sat down to cry again; and by this time the students started coming in, and she had to hide her sadness and broken heart.

Tom ran here and there through the village. Half an hour later he was behind the Douglas mansion atop Cardiff Hill, and the schoolhouse was barely visible.

He went into the center of a dense wood. It was quiet and very lonely. Tom was sad. He sat for a long time with his elbows on his knees and his chin in his hands meditating about Becky.

What had he done? He had meant the best in the world, and been treated like a dog. She would be sorry someday—

maybe when it was too late. What if he turned his back now, and disappeared mysteriously? What if he went far away, into unknown countries, beyond the seas—and never came back! How would she feel then!

But there was something even much better. He would be a pirate! "It's Tom Sawyer—the Pirate—the Black Avenger of the Spanish Main!"

Yes, his career was chosen. He would start the very next morning. He would collect his stuff together.

Tom flung off his jacket and trousers, turned a suspender into a belt, looked behind the rotten log to find a rude bow and arrow, a lath sword, and a tin trumpet, and picked up these things and ran away from there.

CHAPTER 5

The Murder in the Graveyard

At half past nine that night, they said their prayers, and Sid was soon asleep. Tom lay awake and waited. It was midnight! Everything was still. Slowly, little noises began to be heard. The ticking of the clock seemed to get louder. Tom could hear gentle snoring from Aunt Polly's room. Far way in the night, the dogs started howling. Tom was in an agony. Then there came a horrible caterwauling. A window next door was opened, and someone yelled, "Scat! You devil!" A bottle crashed against the back of his aunt's woodshed. A minute later he was dressed and out of the window and creeping along the roof. He jumped to the roof of the woodshed and then to the ground. Huckleberry Finn was there, with his dead cat. The boys moved off into the gloom. In half an hour they were wading through the tall grass of the graveyard.

It was an old-fashioned graveyard on a hill, about a mile and a half from the village. It had a board fence around it, mostly fallen down. Grass and weeds grew all over. All the old graves were sunken in, and many of the tombstones had toppled over.

A faint wind moaned through the trees, and Tom feared it might be the spirits of the dead. They found the new heap that they were seeking, and hid in the three great elms that grew in a bunch.

They waited for what seemed like a long time. An owl hooted somewhere.

Tom whispered, "Huck, do you believe the dead people like it for us to be here?"

Huck whispered, "I wish I knowed."

"I bet they don't."

They thought about this for a while. Then Tom seized Huck's arm, "Shh!"

"What is it, Tom?"

"There! You hear it."

"Tom, they're coming! Sure."

"Look! What is it!" whispered Tom.

"It's devil fire. Tom, this is awful."

Vague figures approached through the gloom, swinging a tin lantern.

Huck whispered, "It's the devils sure. Three of 'em! We're goners! Can you pray?"

"I'll try, but don't you be afeard. They ain't going to hurt us. 'Now I lay me down to sleep, I—' "

"Shh!"

"What is it, Huck?"

"They're humans! One of 'em's old Muff Potter's voice. Don't you stir nor budge. He ain't sharp enough to notice us. Drunk, the same as usual, likely!"

"Say, Huck, it's Injun Joe."

The whispering died out now. The three men had reached the grave and stood very close to the boys' hiding place.

"Here it is," said the third voice; it was young Doctor Robinson.

Potter and Injun Joe were carrying a handbarrow with a rope and a couple of shovels in it. They cast down their load and began to open the grave. The doctor put the lantern close by and sat down with his back against one of the elm trees.

"Hurry, men!" he said. "The moon might come out at any moment."

They growled and went on digging. For some time there was only the grating sound of the spades. Finally a spade struck the coffin, and the men hoisted it out on the ground. They pried off the lid with their shovels, got out the body, and dumped it on the ground. The corpse was placed on the barrow, covered with a blanket, and tied down with the rope.

Potter said, "Now the cussed thing's ready, Sawbones, and you'll just out with another five, or here she stays."

"That's the talk!" said Injun Joe.

"Look here, what does this mean?" said the doctor. "You required your pay in advance, and I've paid you."

"Yes, and you done more than that," said Injun Joe, approaching the doctor, who was now standing. "Five years ago you drove me away from your father's

kitchen one night, when I came to ask for something to eat. You said I wasn't there for any good; and when I swore I'd get even with you if it took a hundred years, your father had me jailed for a vagrant. Did you think I'd forget?"

He was threatening the doctor with his fist in his face, by this time. The doctor struck out suddenly, and the ruffian fell down. Potter dropped his knife and exclaimed, "Here, now, don't you hit my pardner!" and the next moment he was fighting with the doctor. Injun Joe sprang to his feet, snatched up Potter's knife, and went creeping, catlike and stooping, around and around the two men. All at once the doctor pulled himself free, picked up the heavy headboard of Williams's grave, and hit Potter with it—and in the same instant the half-breed saw his chance and stabbed the doctor in the chest. He reeled and fell partly upon Potter, his blood flooding out. Just then, the clouds hid what was going on and the two frightened boys went running away in the dark.

When the moon emerged again, Injun Joe was standing over the two bodies. The doctor murmured, gave a long gasp or two, and was still. The half-breed muttered, "That score is settled—damn you."

Then he robbed the body. After which he put the knife in Potter's open right hand and sat down on the open coffin. Five minutes passed, and then Potter began to stir and moan. His hand closed on the knife; he raised it, looked at it, and let it fall with a shudder. Then he sat up, pushing the body from him, and gazed at it, and then around him, confusedly. His eyes met Joe's.

"What happened, Joe?" he asked.

"It's a dirty business," said Joe.

"What did you do it for?"

"I! I never done it!"

Potter trembled and grew white.

"Why, you two was scuffling, and he fetched you one with the headboard and you fell flat; and then up you come, all reeling and staggering like, and snatched the knife and jammed it into him."

"Oh, I didn't know what I was doing. I wish I may die this minute if I did. It was all on account of the whiskey and the excitement, I reckon. Joe, don't tell! Say you won't tell, Joe—that's a good feller. You won't tell, will you, Joe?" And the poor man dropped on his knees before the murderer and clasped his hands.

"No, you've always been fair and square with me, Muff Potter, and I won't go back on you."

Potter began to cry.

"This ain't any time for blubbering. You be off yonder way and I'll go this way."

Potter ran off. The half-breed stood looking after him. He muttered, "If he's as much stunned and fuddled with rum as he looks, he won't think of the knife

till he's gone so far, he'll be afraid to come back!"

Two or three minutes later the murdered man, the blanketed corpse, the lidless coffin, and the open grave were still under the light of the moon.

The two boys ran toward the village, speechless with horror. They glanced backward over their shoulders from time to time, as if they feared they might be followed. Every stump seemed a man and an enemy; and as they sped by some cottages near the village, the barking of the aroused watchdogs seemed to make them run faster.

"If we can only get to the old tannery before we break down," whispered Tom. "I can't stand it much longer."

Huck's hard pantings were his only reply. The boys ran to an old barn. Tom whispered, "Hucky, what do you reckon'll come of this?"

"If Doctor Robinson dies, I reckon hanging'll come of it."

"Do you, though?"

"Why, I know it, Tom."

Tom said, "Who'll tell? We?"

"What are you talking about? If something happened and Injun Joe didn't hang? Why, he'd kill us some time or other, just as dead sure as we're laying here."

"That's what I was thinking, Huck."

"If anybody tells, let Muff Potter do it, if he's fool enough. He's generally drunk."

After another reflective silence, Tom said, "Hucky, are you sure you can keep mum forever?"

"Tom, we got to keep mum. Let's swear to one another—that's what we got to do—swear to keep mum."

Tom picked up a clean piece of bark, took a little fragment of chalk out of his pocket, and painfully scrawled these lines, his tongue between his teeth:

"Huck Finn and Tom Sawyer swears they will keep mum about this and they may drop down dead in their tracks if they ever tell and rot."

Huckleberry was filled with admiration for Tom's writing. He at once took a pin from his lapel and was going to prick his finger, but Tom unwound the thread from one of his needles, and each boy pricked the ball of his thumb and squeezed out a drop of blood. In time, after many squeezes, Tom managed to sign his initials. Then he showed Huckleberry how to make an H and an F, and the oath was complete. They buried the piece of bark close to the wall, with some incantations.

"Tom," whispered Huckleberry, "does this keep us from ever telling—always?"

"Of course it does. It don't make any difference what happens—we got to keep mum. We'd drop down dead—don't you know that?"

"Yes, I reckon that's so."

When Tom crept in at his bedroom window, the night was almost over. He undressed carefully and fell asleep congratulating himself that nobody knew of his escapade. He did not know that Sid was awake, and had been so for an hour.

When Tom awoke, Sid was dressed and gone. Within five minutes he was dressed and downstairs, feeling sore and drowsy. The family were still at table, but they had finished breakfast. There was no voice of rebuke; but there were averted eyes; there was a silence. Tom sat down and tried to seem normal, but it was not easy.

After breakfast his aunt took him aside. She wept over him and asked him how he could go and break her old heart so; and finally told him to go on, and ruin himself. This was worse than a thousand whippings, and Tom's heart was sorer now than his body. He cried, he pleaded for forgiveness, promised to reform over and over again, and then was sent away.

He left the room too unhappy to even feel angry toward Sid. He moped to school gloomy and sad, and took his flogging, along with Joe Haper, for playing hookey the day before, feeling too miserable to feel anything. He went to his seat, rested his elbows on his desk and his chin in his hands, and stared at the wall. His elbow was pressing against something hard.

After a long time he slowly and sadly changed his position, and picked up this object with a sigh. It was wrapped in paper. He unrolled it. A long, lingering, huge sigh followed, and his heart broke. It was his brass knob!

CHAPTER 6

The Arrest

Around noon, the whole village was electrified with the ghastly news.

A bloody knife had been found close to the body, and someone knew it was Muff Potter's. And then someone saw Potter washing himself in the stream very early in the morning and he had at once sneaked off. This was suspicious, especially since Potter did not like washing.

People drifted toward the graveyard. Tom joined the procession. When he got there, he saw what he had run away from in the night. Somebody pinched his arm. He turned, and his eyes met

Huckleberry's. They both looked else-where, and wondered if anybody had noticed anything.

"Poor young fellow!" "This ought to be a lesson to grave robbers!" "Muff Potter'll hang for this if they catch him!"

Tom shivered; he had seen Injun Joe. At this moment the crowd began to shout, "It's him! It's him! He's coming himself!"

"Who? Who?"

"Muff Potter!"

"Hallo, he's stopped! Look out—he's turning! Don't let him get away!"

The sheriff came leading Potter by the arm. The poor fellow's face was haggard, and his eyes showed his fear. When he stood before the murdered man, he put his face in his hands and burst into tears.

"I didn't do it, friends," he sobbed.

"Is that your knife?" the sheriff asked.

Potter said, "Something told me if I didn't come back and get—" He shuddered, then waved his hand and said, "Tell 'em, Joe, tell 'em—it ain't any use anymore."

Huckleberry and Tom stood dumb and staring, and heard Injun Joe reel off his serene statement. And when he had finished, their impulse vanished. Injun Joe had sold himself to Satan and it would be fatal to meddle with a power like that.

Tom's fearful secret and gnawing conscience disturbed his sleep for as much as a week after this; and at breakfast Sid said, "Tom, you roll around and talk in your sleep so much that you keep me awake half the time."

Tom went pale and dropped his eyes.

"It's a bad sign," said Aunt Polly.

"Nothing I know of," said Tom. But his hand shook and he spilled his coffee.

"And you do talk such stuff," Sid said. "Last night you said, 'It's blood, it's blood!' You said that over and over. And you said, 'Don't torment me so, I'll tell!' Tell what?"

Luckily Aunt Polly came to Tom's rescue without knowing it. She said, "It's that dreadful murder. I dream about it most every night myself."

Mary said she had been affected much the same way. Sid seemed satisfied.

Tom got out of there as quick as he could, and then he complained of toothache for a week and tied up his jaws every night. He never knew that Sid lay watching, and frequently slipped the bandage off and then leaned on his elbow listening, and afterward slipped the bandage back on again. Tom's distress wore off gradually. If Sid really managed to make anything out of Tom's mutterings, he kept it to himself.

Every day Tom went to the jail and

smuggled small comforts through to Potter. This helped to ease Tom's conscience.

Around this time, Becky Thatcher stopped coming to school. Tom tried to find her, but failed. He began to hang around her father's house at night. She was ill. What if she died! He was no longer interested in war, or even piracy. The charm of life was gone. His aunt was concerned. She began to try and fix him.

Aunty Polly liked trying out any new cure that she could find. The water treatment was new now, and Tom's condition was perfect for her to test it on him. She woke him up at daylight every morning, stood him in the woodshed, and drowned him with buckets of cold water; then she scrubbed him down with a rough towel; then she rolled him up in a wet sheet and put him under blankets till she sweated his soul clean.

But still the boy got sadder and paler.

Nothing worked. She fed him oatmeal. And she did lots more.

But Tom didn't react to anything. Aunt Polly read about Pain-killer and ordered a lot. She tasted it and was thankful. It was fire in a liquid form. She stopped her treatments and gave Tom a teaspoonful of Pain-killer and watched anxiously for the result. Her troubles were instantly over, her soul at peace again; Tom was fine again.

Tom felt that it was time to wake up. So he thought about various plans for finding amusement, and finally decided to say that he liked Pain-killer. He asked for it so often that he became a nuisance, so his aunt told him to help himself and stop bothering her. She watched the bottle carefully and found that the medicine did really get drunk. But she never found out that Tom was pouring it into a crack in the sitting-room floor.

One day Tom was doing just this

when his aunt's yellow cat came along, purring, looking at it, and begging for a taste.

Tom said, "Don't ask for it unless you want it, Peter."

But Peter did want it.

"You better make sure."

Peter was sure.

"Now you've asked for it, I'll give it to you. But if you don't like it, you mustn't blame anybody but yourself."

Peter agreed. So Tom pried his mouth open and poured in some Pain-killer. Peter leaped up in the air, yelled a war whoop, and ran around and around the room, banging against furniture, upsetting flower pots, going mad. Then he went tearing around the house again. Aunt Polly came in just in time to see him do a few double somersaults, yell one final time, and sail through the open window, upsetting the flower pots. The old lady stood there, astonished, peering over her glasses; Tom lay on the floor laughing.

"Tom, what on earth is wrong with that cat?"

"I don't know, Aunt," gasped the boy.

The old lady was bending down, Tom watching with interest and a little worry. The handle of the teaspoon was visible under the bed. Aunt Polly held it up. Tom looked down. Aunt Polly pulled him up by the ear and tapped him hard on the head with her thimble. "Now, why did you do that to the cat?"

"I done it out of pity for him—because he hadn't any aunt."

"Hadn't any aunt! What's that got to do with it?"

"Lots. Because if he had one, she'd have tortured him!"

Aunt Polly felt suddenly sorry for what she had done. What was cruelty to a cat might be cruelty to a boy, too. She felt sorry. Her eyes watered a little, and she put her hand on Tom's head and said gently, "I was meaning for the best, Tom. And, Tom, it did do you good."

Tom looked up in her face with just a little twinkle in his eye.

"I know you meant for the best, Aunty, and so did I with Peter. It done him good, too. I never see him go so fast—"

"Oh, Tom! You try and see if you can't be a good boy, for once, and you needn't take any more medicine."

Tom reached school ahead of time. This had been happening every day now. He hung about the gate of the schoolyard instead of playing with his friends. He was sick, he said. He tried to seem as if he was looking everywhere except where he was really looking— down the road. Tom watched—hoping whenever he saw a frock, and hating the owner of it as soon as he saw she was not the right one. At last the road was empty and he went into the empty

schoolhouse. Then one more frock passed, and Tom's heart leaped.

The next instant he was out doing all the heroic things. But Becky never looked. He went closer to her and fell sprawling under Becky's nose. She turned, with her nose in the air, and he heard her say, "Mff! Some people think they're smart, always showing off!"

Tom's cheeks burned. He got up and sneaked off, crushed and crestfallen.

CHAPTER 7

The Pirates Set Sail

Tom was gloomy and desperate. He had no friends, he said; nobody loved him. He would lead a life of crime. There was no choice.

Just then he met Joe Harper, hard-eyed. Tom began to blubber something about meaning to escape by roaming around the world, never to return. This was just what Joe was going to request of Tom. His mother had whipped him for drinking cream that he had never tasted.

The two boys walked along sadly. Then they began to make plans. Joe wanted to be a hermit, living on crusts in a cave; but after listening to Tom, he

73

said that a life of crime would be good, too, and so he agreed to be a pirate.

Three miles below St. Petersburg, where the Mississippi River was just over a mile wide, there was a long, narrow, wooded island, which was a perfect meeting point. No one lived there, and parts of it were covered with thick forest. So they chose Jackson's Island. Then they hunted up Huckleberry Finn, and he joined them. They decided to meet at a lonely spot on the riverbank at midnight.

About midnight Tom arrived with a boiled ham and some other stuff to eat. The mighty river was still. Then Tom gave a low whistle, which was answered from under the bluff. Then a voice said, "Who goes there?"

"Tom Sawyer, the Black Avenger of the Spanish Main. Who are you?"

"Huck Finn the Red-Handed, and Joe Harper, the Terror of the Seas."

"Give the countersign."

Two hoarse whispers said the same awful word together: "Blood!"

The Terror of the Seas had brought a side of bacon. Finn the Red-Handed had stolen a skillet and a quantity of half-cured leaf tobacco, and had also brought a few corncobs to make pipes with. But only he smoked or "chewed." The Black Avenger of the Spanish Main said they had to have a fire. They saw a fire smoldering a hundred yards above them and they sneaked up there and helped themselves to a chunk.

They found a raft and shoved off, Tom in command, Huck at the after oar and Joe at the forward. Tom stood there gloomy, with folded arms, and gave his orders.

About two o'clock in the morning the raft grounded on the bar two hundred yards above the head of the island, and they unloaded it. They had an old sail

and they spread it over some bushes to make a tent to store their food, but they themselves would sleep in the open air.

They built a fire and cooked some bacon in the frying pan for supper. When the last crisp slice of bacon was gone and the last bite of corn "pone" eaten up, the boys stretched out on the grass.

"It's just the life for me," said Tom. "You don't have to get up mornings, and you don't have to go to school, and wash, and all that silly stuff. You see, a pirate don't have to do anything, Joe."

"Oh, yes," said Joe. "I'd rather be a pirate, now that I've tried it."

Gradually their talk faded away as they started falling asleep. The Red-Handed dropped his pipe and slept peacefully. The Terror of the Seas and the Black Avenger of the Spanish Main found it more difficult to sleep. They said their prayers to themselves, lying down.

When Tom woke up in the morning, he wondered where he was. Slowly, the morning grew.

The sun came out, the birds started singing, and the bugs and worms started going about their business. A brown-spotted ladybug climbed up a grass blade, and Tom bent down close to it and said, "Ladybug, ladybug, fly away home, your house is on fire, your children's alone," and she flew away. A catbird, the Northern mocker, landed in a tree over Tom's head, and trilled joyfully. A gray squirrel and a big fox kind came running past, not afraid, since they had not seen people before.

Tom woke up his friends. And they all ran to the water for a swim. They didn't feel like going home. Their raft was gone, probably floating down the river, and that made them feel like they had truly left their old lives behind.

They came back to their camp fresh and happy, very hungry, so they drank cold water from cups made of leaves, which made the water taste so much better. Joe started slicing bacon for breakfast, but Tom and Huck asked him to wait—they would try their luck fishing. And sure enough, they soon had a lot of fish and ate it with bacon for breakfast. Then, after a short lie-down, they went to explore the island.

They discovered that the island was about three miles long and a quarter of a mile wide, and was just about two hundred yards away from the mainland at one point; they could easily swim over. And they swam a lot—every hour or so, until it was lunchtime. They sat there and chatted, but soon, as they slowly ran out of things to talk about, they started feeling lonely and missed home. But none of them was brave enough to say so.

For some time now the boys had vaguely heard a strange sound far way. Now it was louder. A deep, sullen boom came floating to their ears.

"What is it!" exclaimed Joe.

"I wonder," said Tom in a whisper.

"Isn't thunder," said Huckleberry, in an awed tone.

Tom said, "Listen—don't talk."

The sound came again.

"Let's go and see."

They ran to the shore and peered out to where they could see the village. The little steam ferryboat was about a mile below the village, drifting with the current. Her broad deck was crowded with people. Many skiffs were rowing about or floating in the neighborhood of the ferryboat, but the boys couldn't see properly what they were doing. Suddenly, a great jet of white smoke burst from the ferryboat's side, and that same dull sound was heard.

"I know now!" exclaimed Tom. "Somebody's drowned!"

"That's it!" said Huck. "They did that last summer, when Bill Turner got drowned; they shot a cannon over the water, and that made him come up to the top."

"By jings, I wish I was over there, now," said Joe.

"I do, too," said Huck. "I'd give heaps to know who it is."

The boys listened and watched. Presently a thought flashed through Tom's mind, and he exclaimed, "Boys, I know who's drowned—it's us!"

They felt like heroes in an instant. Here was a triumph: They were missed;

hearts were breaking for them; people were crying for them; and everyone was sorry that they had been unkind to them.

This was fine. It was worthwhile to be a pirate after all.

As it got dark, the ferryboat went back and the pirates returned to their camp.

Huck began to nod, and soon to snore. Joe followed. Tom lay there for a while, not moving, watching them. At last he got up carefully, on his knees, and went searching in the grass.

He found two pieces of white bark that he liked and wrote something on them with his red pencil; one he rolled up and put in his jacket pocket, and the other he put in Joe's hat. He also put into the hat some of his

treasures—a lump of chalk, an India rubber ball, three fishhooks, and a very special marble. Then he tiptoed his way into the trees. When he was far enough away that the others would not hear, he started running toward the sandbar that was so close to his home.

CHAPTER 8

Tom Visits Home

A few minutes later Tom was swimming toward the mainland. He reached the shore finally. He pulled himself out. He put his hand on his jacket pocket, found his piece of bark safe, and then walked through the woods, soaking wet, to the village.

He soon found himself at his aunt's back fence. He climbed over, and saw Aunt Polly, Sid, Mary, and Joe Harper's mother, talking. They were by the bed, and the bed was between them and the door. Tom went to the door and began to push it softly, gently open.

"What makes the candle blow?" said

Aunt Polly. "Go and shut the door, Sid."

Tom slid himself under the bed just in time. "Tom wasn't bad, only mischievous," Aunt Polly said, and began to cry.

"Just so with my Joe, always up to every kind of mischief!" And Mrs. Harper sobbed as if her heart would break.

"Yes, Mrs. Harper, I know just exactly how you feel."

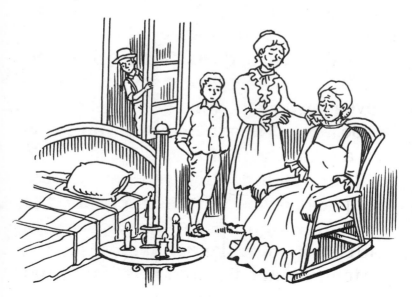

Tom went on listening, and understood that people thought at first that the boys had drowned while taking a swim; then the raft had been missed. The wise heads thought that the lads had gone off on that raft and would turn up at the next town; but toward noon the raft had been found, and then hope perished. They might have drowned, else they would have come home by nightfall. If the bodies were not found by Sunday, the funerals would be held that morning. Tom shuddered.

Mrs. Harper sobbed Good night. Then, the two bereaved women flung themselves into each other's arms and had a good cry, and parted. Sid snuffled a bit, and Mary went off crying.

It took a long time for Aunt Polly to be completely asleep. But at last she was still, and Tom shaded the candlelight with his hand and stood looking at her. He took out his note and placed it by the candle. But then something changed his mind—he put the note back in his pocket, bent over and kissed his aunt, and made his exit, latching the door behind him.

Tom walked tiredly to the camp. Just as he got there, he heard Joe say, "No, Tom's true-blue, Huck, and he'll come back. He's up to something or other. His note says these things are ours if he ain't back here to breakfast."

"Which he is!" exclaimed Tom.

A big breakfast of bacon and fish was eaten, and Tom told his friends just what he had been up to. Then he hid himself away in a shady nook to sleep till noon.

After dinner the gang went to hunt for turtle eggs. They had a fried-egg feast that night, and another on Friday.

After breakfast they played in the water. When they were exhausted, they would run out and sprawl on the dry, hot sand, until they were ready to go in the water again.

Soon the boys were tired. They lay on the sand, gazing longingly across the wide river to where the village was. Tom found himself writing "BECKY" in the sand. He scratched it out and was angry with himself for writing it. But he wrote it again; he could not help it. And then he erased it and went back to play.

But Joe was so homesick that he could hardly bear it. Huck was depressed,

too. Neither was Tom happy, but he tried hard not to show it. He had a secret that he was not ready to tell yet, but if they kept on being gloomy and unhappy, he would have to bring it out. He said, "I bet there's been pirates on this island before, boys. We'll explore it again. They've hid treasures here somewhere."

But no one was interested in what Tom had to tell them. Finally, Joe said, "I want to go home. It's so lonesome."

Tom was uneasy, too. Joe began to wade off toward the far shore.

Huck said, "I want to go, too, Tom. It was getting so lonesome, anyway, and now it'll be worse. Let us go, too, Tom."

"I won't! You can all go, if you want to. I mean to stay."

Huck said, "Tom, I wish you'd come, too. Now you think it over. We'll wait for you when we get to shore."

"Well, you'll wait for long, that's all."

Huck started off and Tom stood look-ing after him, wanting to go, too, but too proud to join his friends. He suddenly found that it was becoming very lonely. He then darted after his friends, yelling, "I want to tell you something!"

They stopped and turned around. Tom began telling his secret, and they listened till at last they saw the point he was driving at and then they whooped madly and said it was wonderful and if

he had told them before, they wouldn't have started for home.

The lads went back to their fun, chattering all the time about Tom's plan and admiring the genius of it.

But there was something in the air that was not right. The boys huddled themselves together around the fire. They sat still, intent and waiting. The solemn hush continued. Beyond the light of the fire everything was swallowed up in the blackness. Gradually, the storm began, first with lightning, then thunder, then the wind and the rain. It was cold rain.

"Quick! boys, go for the tent!" exclaimed Tom.

They ran, stumbling over roots and vines in the dark. One blinding flash after another came, and peal upon peal of deafening thunder. And a drenching rain poured down and the wind drove it in sheets along the ground. One by one the boys straggled into the tent and took shelter, cold, scared, and streaming with water. They could not talk, there was too much noise outside. The storm grew so fierce that soon the tent blew away. The boys grabbed one another's hands and ran, with many falls and bruises, to the shelter of a great oak on the riverbank. It was a wild night for homeless young boys to be out in.

At last the storm ended. The boys went back to their camp.

As the sun rose in the morning, the boys found that they were very sleepy, so they went out on the sandbar and lay down. It was very hot and they were getting sunburned, so they went off to get breakfast. They felt rusty and stiff, and a little homesick once more. Tom started cheering up the pirates as well as he could. He reminded them of the secret, and that made them think happy thoughts for a little while.

CHAPTER 9

Tom's Great Secret

The village was not a happy place on Sunday. The Harpers and Aunt Polly's family were in mourning.

In the afternoon Becky found herself feeling very low. But she found nothing there to comfort her. She said to herself, "If I only had a brass knob again! I haven't got anything now to remember him by." And she choked back a little sob. "It was right here. Oh, if I could do it all over again, I wouldn't say that for the whole world. But he's gone now. I'll never see him anymore."

That thought made her cry. Then a group of boys and girls, Tom's and

Joe's friends, came by and stood talking about the last time they saw them.

When Sunday School was finished, the bell began to toll. The villagers began to gather, whispering about the sad event. Aunt Polly entered with Sid and Mary, and then the Harper family, all in deep black. The whole congregation rose and stood until the mourners were seated in the front pew. They all sang a hymn, and read the text "I am the Resurrection and the Life."

The clergyman told many touching stories about the three lads, which showed their sweet, generous natures. Everyone was in tears, the preacher himself crying in the pulpit.

Nobody noticed the noise in the gallery. Suddenly the church door creaked open. The three dead boys came marching up the aisle, Tom in the lead, Joe next, and Huck sneaking in the rear! They had hid in the unused gallery listening to their own funeral sermon!

Aunt Polly, Mary, and the Harpers grabbed their children, smothered them with kisses, and thanked God, while poor Huck stood there not knowing where to hide from so many people staring at him.

Tom held Huck by his hand and said, "Aunt Polly, somebody's got to be glad to see Huck."

"I'm glad to see him!" Aunt Polly said.

And the loving attentions Huck got from Aunt Polly made him more uncomfortable than before.

The minister shouted at the top of his voice, "Praise God from whom all blessings flow—sing! And put your hearts in it!"

That was Tom's great secret: to return home with his brother pirates and attend their own funerals.

At breakfast Monday morning, Aunt Polly and Mary were very loving to Tom.

Aunt Polly said, "Well, I don't say it wasn't a fine joke, Tom, to keep everybody suffering 'most a week so you boys had a good time, but it is a pity you could be so hard-hearted as to let me suffer so. If you could come over on a log to go to your funeral, you could have come over and given me a hint that you weren't dead but only run off."

"Yes, you could have done that, Tom," said Mary. "And I believe you would

have if you had thought of it."

"Tom, I hoped you loved me that much," said Aunt Polly. "It would have been something if you'd cared enough to think of it, even if you didn't do it."

"Now, Auntie, you know I do care for you," said Tom.

"I'd know it better if you acted more like it."

"I wish now I'd thought," said Tom, with a repentant tone. "But I dreamed about you, anyway. That's something, ain't it?"

"It ain't much—a cat does that much—but it's better than nothing. What did you dream?"

"Why, Wednesday night I dreamed that you were sitting over there by the bed, and Sid was sitting by the wood-box, and Mary next to him."

"And I dreamed that Joe Harper's mother was here. Somehow it seems to me that the wind—the wind blowed the candle! And it seems to me that you said, 'Why, I believe that that door'— oh, yes, you said you believed the door was open. And then—and then—well I won't be certain, but it seems like as if you made Sid go and—and—you made him—you—oh, you made him shut it. Oh, it's all getting just as bright as day, now. Next you said I wasn't bad, only mischievous, and not any more responsible than—than—I think it was a colt, or something."

"And so it was! Well, goodness gracious! Go on, Tom!"

"And then you began to cry."

"So I did. So I did. Not the first time, neither. And then—"

"Then Mrs. Harper began to cry, and said Joe was just the same. And then Sid said—I think he said—I think he hoped I was better off where I was gone to, but if I'd been better sometimes—and you shut him up sharp."

"I did!"

"And then there was a whole lot of talk 'bout dragging the river for us, and 'bout having the funeral Sunday, and then you and old Miss Harper hugged and cried, and she went."

"It happened just so!"

"Then I thought you prayed for me. And you went to bed, and I was so sorry that I took and wrote on a piece of sycamore bark, 'We ain't dead—we are only off being pirates,' and put it on the table by the candle; and then you looked so good, lying there asleep, that I thought I went and leaned over and kissed you."

"Did you, Tom! I just forgive you!" And Aunt Polly hugged him.

At school the children made so much of him and of Joe, and praised them so much, that the two heroes were fast becoming stuck-up. They began to tell their adventures to everyone—each time, with more color added.

Tom decided that he could be independent of Becky Thatcher now. Glory was sufficient. Now that he was famous, maybe she would want to make up. Well, let her—she should see that he was not interested anymore. Soon she came to school. Tom pretended not to see her. But then he observed that she was laughing and playing and running with her friends, always in his vicinity. He also noticed that she looked at him sideways, from the corner of her eyes. Then she observed that Tom was talking more to Amy Lawrence than to anyone else. She felt a sharp pang and grew uneasy. She tried to go away, but her feet carried her to the group instead. Tom was telling Amy about the terrible storm on the island, and how the lightning tore the great sycamore tree while he was "standing within three feet of it."

Then Tom turned away, still talking, and took Amy with him. Becky's lips trembled and the tears came to her eyes; she went on chattering, but all she wanted to do was cry.

At recess Tom continued his flirtation with Amy. And he kept drifting about, looking for Becky. At last he spied her, but his heart fell. She was sitting cosily on a little bench behind the school-

house looking at a picture book with Alfred Temple. Tom was very jealous. He began to hate himself for ignoring Becky. He did not hear what Amy was saying. Becky noticed and knew that she had Tom still, but wanted him to suffer a little, like she had suffered.

Tom fled home at noon. His could not watch Becky with Alfred any longer and was fed up with Amy's chatter. Becky was also miserable and said sharply to Alfred, "Oh, don't bother me!" and burst into tears, got up, and walked away.

Alfred went into the deserted schoolhouse. He was angry. He knew that Becky was just trying to teach Tom a lesson. He wished there was some way to get that boy into trouble without much risk to himself. He saw Tom's spelling book. Here was his chance. He opened it to the lesson for the afternoon and poured ink on the page.

Becky, glancing in at a window, saw it

happen, and moved on, quietly.

She wanted to find Tom and tell him; Tom would be thankful, and their troubles would be over. But before she was halfway home, she had changed her mind. She was still angry with Tom. She decided to let him get whipped for the spelling book, and to hate him forever.

CHAPTER 10

Tom Gets Caught

When Tom arrived at home, the first thing his aunt said to him was, "Tom, I've a notion to skin you alive!"

"Auntie, what have I done?"

"Well, you've done enough. Here I go over to Sereny Harper, like an old softy, expecting I'm going to make her believe all that stuff about your dream, but she told me that she'd found out from Joe that you was over here and heard all the talk we had that night. Tom, I don't know what is to become of a boy that will act like that."

Tom hung his head and could not think of anything to say for a moment.

107

Then he said, "Auntie, I wish I hadn't done it—but I didn't think. I know now it was mean, but I didn't mean to be mean. And, besides, I didn't come over here to laugh at you that night."

"What did you come for, then?"

"It was to tell you not to be uneasy about us, because we hadn't got drowned."

"Tom, I would be the most thankful soul in this world if I could believe you ever had as good a thought as that, but you know you never did—and I know it."

"Indeed I did, Auntie."

"Oh, Tom, don't lie."

"It ain't a lie, Auntie. It's the truth. I wanted to keep you from grieving—that was all that made me come."

"Why didn't you tell me, Tom?"

"Why, you see, when you got to talking about the funeral, I just got the idea of our coming and hiding in the church. I couldn't somehow bear to spoil it. So I just put the bark back in my pocket and kept mum."

"What bark?"

"The bark I had wrote on to tell you we'd gone pirating. I wish, now, you'd woken up when I kissed you—I do, honest."

The hard lines in his aunt's face relaxed, and a sudden tenderness dawned in her eyes. "Did you kiss me, Tom?"

"Why, yes, I did."

"What did you kiss me for, Tom?"

"Because I loved you so, and you laid there moaning and I was so sorry."

The moment he was gone, she ran to a closet and got out the ruin of a jacket that Tom had gone pirating in. Then she stopped, with it in her hand, and said to herself, "Poor boy, I reckon he's lied about it—but it's a blessed, blessed lie. I hope the Lord—I know the Lord will forgive him because it was the good-heartedness in him that made him tell it."

She put the jacket away, and stood thinking. She put out her hand to take the jacket and stopped. Then she told herself, "It's a good lie. I won't let it upset me." So she looked in the jacket pocket and found Tom's piece of bark. She began to cry. "I could forgive the

boy, now, if he'd committed a million sins!"

There was something about Aunt Polly's manner, when she kissed Tom, that made him happy again. He started walking to school and had the luck of meeting Becky at the Meadow Lane. Without any hesitation he ran to her and said, "I acted mighty mean, Becky, and I'm so sorry. I won't ever do that way again, as long as ever I live—please make up, won't you?"

The girl stopped and looked at him scornfully. "Mr. Thomas Sawyer. I'll never speak to you again."

She walked away. Tom was so stunned that he could not say anything. But he was angry. He wished she were a boy, because he could hit her then. He presently met her and said something nasty as he passed. She said something back, and the fight was on. Becky was so angry that she wanted to see Tom punished for the ink-stained spelling book. She had forgotten all about Alfred doing it.

But she was walking into trouble herself! The master, Mr. Dobbins, every day took the book out of his desk and read it when he did not have to mind the class. He kept that book locked up, and everyone wanted to peek at it.

Now, as Becky was passing by the

desk, she noticed that the key was in the lock! She glanced around, found herself alone, and the next instant she had the book in her hands. The title page, Professor Somebody's anatomy, told her nothing; she began to turn the pages. The first thing she saw was the colored picture of a human figure, stark naked. At that moment Tom stepped in at the door and caught a glimpse of the picture. Becky tried to close the book, but in her hurry the page tore down the middle. She shoved the book into the desk, turned the key, and burst out crying with shame.

"You ought to be ashamed of yourself, Tom Sawyer. You know you're going to tell on me, and oh, what shall I do! I'll be whipped." She ran out crying.

In a few moments the master arrived and class began. Every time Tom peeked at Becky, her face troubled him. When the spelling book was found to have ink spilled on it, Tom's mind was full of his own troubles for a while. Becky did not expect that Tom could get out of it by denying that he had spilled the ink on the book himself; and she was right. When the worst happened, she wanted to get up and tell on Alfred Temple, but she forced herself to keep still— because, said she to herself, He'll tell about me tearing the picture. I wouldn't say a word, not to save his life!

Tom took his whipping and went back to his seat not too upset. He thought it was possible that he had upset the ink on the spelling book himself when he was playing; he could not remember.

A whole hour drifted by. By and by, Mr. Dobbins sat up, yawned; unlocked his desk and reached for his book, then took it out and started reading! Tom looked at Becky. She looked like a hunted and helpless rabbit with a gun at its head. Instantly he forgot his quarrel with her. Quick—something must be done! He would run and snatch the book, spring through the door, and fly. Too late. There was no help for Becky now. The next moment the master faced the school. There was silence. Then Mr. Dobbins spoke, "Who tore this book?"

There was not a sound. One could have heard a pin drop.

"Rebecca Thatcher"—her face was white with terror—"did you tear—no, look me in the face"—her hands rose in

appeal—"did you tear this book?"

Tom sprang to his feet and shouted, "I done it!"

The school stared. Tom stood a moment; and when he stepped forward to get his punishment, the surprise, the gratitude, the adoration that shone out of poor Becky's eyes seemed pay enough for a hundred floggings.

He took the most merciless flaying that Mr. Dobbins had ever given without even a whimper; and he faced the punishment of having to remain two hours after school was dismissed—he knew who would wait for him outside till he was free.

Tom went to bed that night planning revenge against Alfred Temple; Becky had told him everything. But Tom had more happy thoughts to think about, and he fell asleep at last with Becky's words lingering in his ear: "Tom, how could you be so noble!"

CHAPTER 11

The Revival

Vacation was approaching. The schoolmaster grew more strict and punished the students as he wanted a good showing on "Examination Day." At last they schemed a plan. They swore the village sign painter's boy told him the scheme and asked for his help.

The exciting day arrived. In the evening the schoolhouse was brightly lit up and decorated with flowers. The master sat in his great chair on a raised platform. In front of him sat important people from the town and the parents of the students. Behind the people sat the students who were to take part in the exercises.

Then there were more poems, reading exercises, and a spelling bee.

The happy master turned his back to the audience and began to draw a map of America on the blackboard, to show off what the geography class had learned. But he had drunk a little wine and his hand was unsteady.

There was a garret above, with an opening over his head, and down through this hole came a cat, suspended by a string; she had a rag tied around her head and jaws to keep her from mewing. When she was about six inches from the teacher's head—down, a little lower, she grabbed his wig with her claws, clung to it, and was snatched up into the garret! And the light blazed from the master's bald head—the sign painter's boy had gilded it!

The boys were avenged.

Vacation had come. Becky Thatcher was at her parents' Constantinople home for her vacation, so there was no bright side to life anywhere.

The dreadful secret of the murder was a misery that refused to go away. Then came the measles.

For two long weeks Tom lay dead to the world and its happenings. When he got up at last and went out, everything had changed.

119

There had been a "revival," and everybody had "got religion." Tom hoped to see one blessed sinful face, but couldn't find any. He found Joe Harper studying a Testament. Ben Rogers was visiting the poor. Jim Hollis said Tom should see his measles as a warning. In desperation, he looked for Huckleberry Finn and was recited a quote from the Scriptures. Tom's heart broke and he

went home.

At last the village woke up. The murder trial was in the court. All of the village could talk about nothing else. Every word about the murder shook Tom with fear. He met Huck at a lonely place.

"Huck, have you ever told anybody about—that?"

"Oh—'course I haven't."

"Never a word?"

"Never a solitary word."

"Well, I was afraid."

"Why, Tom, we wouldn't be alive two days if that got found out."

"Well, that's all right. I reckon we're safe as long as we keep mum."

So they swore again.

"What is the talk around, Huck?"

"Talk? Well, it's just Muff Potter, Muff Potter, all the time."

"I've heard 'em say that if he was to get free, they'd lynch him."

The boys had a long talk, but it brought them little comfort. The boys did as they had often done before—went to the cell grating and gave Potter some tobacco and matches. He was on the ground floor and there were no guards.

CHAPTER 12

Muff Potter's Trial in the Court

All the village went to the courthouse the next morning. After a long wait the jury filed in and took their places. Soon Potter, pale and haggard, timid and hopeless, was brought in. Injun Joe was also there, stolid as ever. The judge arrived, and the sheriff announced the opening of the court. A witness said that he found Muff Potter washing in the brook. After some questions, counsel for the prosecution said, "By the oaths of citizens, we have found, beyond all possibility of doubt, the prisoner at the bar guilty. We rest our case here."

A groan escaped from poor Potter, and

he put his face in his hands. Counsel for the defense rose and said, "Your Honor, in our remarks at the opening of this trial, we wished to establish that our client did this fearful deed under the influence of the drink." Then he turned to the clerk and said, "Call Thomas Sawyer!"

Everyone was puzzled. Every eye gazed upon Tom as he rose and took his place on the stand. The oath was administered.

"Thomas Sawyer, where were you on the seventeenth of June, at midnight?"

Tom glanced at Injun Joe's iron face and found himself tongue-tied. After a few moments, however, the boy got a little of his strength back. "In the graveyard!"

"Were you anywhere near Horse Williams's grave?"

"Yes, sir."

"Speak up. How near were you?"

"Near as I am to you."

"Were you hidden, or not?"

"I was hid, behind the elms on the edge of the grave."

Injun Joe gave a perceptible start.

In a while every sound stopped but Tom's—"and as the doctor fetched the board around and Muff Potter fell, Injun Joe jumped with the knife and fled

away."

As a result of Tom's testimony, Muff Potter was set free. Tom's days were wonderful, but his nights were horrible. Injun Joe appeared in all his dreams. Huck was in the same state. Tom had told the whole story to the lawyer the night before the great day of the trial. He was afraid that his share in the business might leak out.

Tom was sure he could never be safe again until that man was dead and he had seen the corpse.

CHAPTER 13

The Haunted House

There comes a time in every boy's life when he must go somewhere and dig for hidden treasure. This happened to Tom one day. He couldn't find Joe Harper or Ben Rogers. Presently he met Huck Finn. Tom told him about his idea in confidence. Huck was willing. Huck was always willing to do anything that was fun and needed no money. "Where'll we dig?" asked Huck.

"Oh, anywhere."

They got a pick and a shovel and set out. They arrived hot and panting, and stopped in the shade of an elm to rest.

They dug for half an hour, but no

result. They dug another half an hour. Still, no result. So they chose a new spot and began again. Finally Huck leaned on his shovel, wiped his face, and said, "Say, Tom, let's give this place up and try somewheres else."

The boys went digging that night. They sat in the shadow waiting. It was a lonely place. Spirits whispered in the rustling leaves, the deep baying of a hound floated up out of the distance, an owl answered. The boys were subdued, and talked little. By and by they judged that twelve had come; they marked

where the shadow fell, and began to dig.

At last Tom said, "What'll it be?"

Tom considered awhile; and then said, "The ha'nted house. That's it!"

They had started down the hill by this time. There in the middle of the moonlit valley below them stood the "haunted" house. The boys gazed awhile, half expecting to see a blue light flit past a window; then they went far off to the right, way around the haunted house, and walked homeward through the woods.

On Saturday, the boys were at the dead tree again. They dug a little in their last hole, because Tom said that people had often given up a treasure after getting within six inches of it, and then somebody else had come along and turned it up. This time it didn't happen, so the boys picked up their tools and went away.

When they reached the haunted house

there was dead silence, so they were
afraid to go in. Then they crept to the
door and peeped in. They saw a weed-

grown, floorless room, an ancient fireplace, vacant windows, and a ruined staircase. They went in, ready to run out.

But they got used to it soon enough. Next they went upstairs. Up there were the same ruins. They were about to go down and begin work when—

"Shh!" said Tom.

"What is it?" whispered Huck, pale with fright. "Yes! Oh, my! Let's run!"

"Keep still! Don't you budge! They're coming right toward the door."

The boys lay on the floor with their eyes to holes in the planks.

Two men came in. The boys thought, There's the old deaf and dumb Spaniard that's been about town once or twice lately—never saw the other man before.

"The other man" was a ragged, unkempt creature. The Spaniard was wrapped in a serape. He had bushy white whiskers, long white hair, and he wore green goggles. When they came in, "the other" was talking in a low voice. They sat down on the ground.

"No," said he, "I've thought it all over, and I don't like it. It's dangerous."

"Dangerous!" grunted the "deaf and dumb" Spaniard—to the vast surprise of the boys. "Milksop!"

It was Injun Joe!

The two men started eating. Then Injun Joe said, "You go back up the river. Wait there till you hear from me."

Both men yawned, and Injun Joe said, "It's your turn to watch."

He soon began to snore. His friend stirred him once or twice and presently fell asleep. Both men snored now.

Tom whispered, "Now's our chance!"

Huck said, "I can't—I'd die if they were to wake up."

Tom urged—Huck held back. At last Tom rose slowly and softly, and started alone. But the first step made the floor creak so loudly that he sank down almost dead with fright. He never tried again. The boys lay there waiting; and then they saw that at last the sun was setting.

Then Injun Joe sat up, stared around— and kicked his friend awake.

"Here! You're a watchman, ain't you? All right, though—nothing's happened."

"My! have I been asleep?"

"Oh, partly, partly. Nearly time for us to be moving. What'll we do with what little swag we've got left?"

"I don't know—leave it here, as we've always done, I reckon. No use to take it away till we start south. Six hundred and fifty in silver's something to carry."

"We'll just bury it really deep."

The friend who walked across the room, knelt raised one of the back hearth stones and took out a bag that jingled. He took twenty or thirty dollars for himself and that much for Injun Joe, and the two men started to bury the bag.

Joe's knife struck something as he dug.

"Hello!" said he. "Half-rotten plank—no, it's a box, I believe."

He reached his hand in and drew it out—"Man, it's money!"

The two men examined the gold coins. Joe's friend said, "There's an old rusty pick in the weeds in the corner there."

He ran and brought the boys' pick and shovel. Injun Joe took the pick, looked it over, shook his head, and then began to dig. The box was not very large. The men gazed at the treasure in happy silence.

"Pard', there's thousands of dollars here," said Injun Joe.

"What'll we do—bury it again?"

"Yes. No! That pick had fresh earth on it! What business has a pick and a shovel here? What business with fresh earth on them? Who brought them here? We can't bury this. We'll take it to my den."

"Why, yes! You mean Number One?"

"No—Number Two—under the cross."

Soon they slipped out of the house and moved toward the river with the box.

Tom and Huck rose and stared after them through the chinks between the logs of the house. They both thought that they should not have brought their tools there—Injun Joe never would have suspected if he had not seen the pick and shovel. He would have hidden the silver with the gold to wait there till his "revenge" was satisfied.

They resolved to keep a lookout for that Spaniard and follow him to "Number Two." Then Tom said, "Revenge? What if he means us, Huck?"

CHAPTER 14

The Hidden Treasure

That night, Tom dreamed about the adventure they had had that day. Four times he'd had his hands on that rich treasure and four times he woke up. When he woke up in the morning, everything seemed very far away.

But as he thought about it, what happened the day before seemed more likely and not a dream. He had to be sure. He would ask Huck. Tom decided to let Huck start talking about it. That would show that it was not a dream.

"Hello, Huck."

"Hello, Tom. If we'd left the blame tools at the dead tree, we'd got the money."

"'Tain't a dream! Somehow I most wish it was. Dog'd if I don't, Huck."

"What ain't a dream?"

"Oh, that thing yesterday."

"I've had dreams enough all night—with that Spanish devil going for me all through 'em!"

"Find him! Track the money!"

"Tom, we'll never find him. A feller don't have only one chance for such a pile—and that one's lost. I'd feel mighty

shaky if I was to see him, anyway."

"Well, so'd I; but I'd like to see him and track him out—to his Number 2."

"Number 2—yes, that's it. I been thinking 'bout that. I can't make nothing out of it. What do you reckon it is?"

"I dunno. It's too deep. Say, Huck—maybe it's the number of a house!"

"No, Tom, that ain't it. They ain't no numbers here."

"Well, that's so. Here—it's the number of a room—in a tavern, you know!"

"Oh, that's the trick! They ain't only two taverns. We can find out quick."

Tom was off at once. He found that in the best tavern, No. 2 was occupied by a young lawyer. In another inn, No. 2 was a mystery. The tavern keeper's young son said it was kept locked all the time, and he never saw anybody go into it or come out of it except at night. He ran to Huck.

"That's what I've found out, Huck. I

reckon that's the very No. 2 we're after."

"I reckon it is, Tom. Now what you going to do?"

Tom thought a long time. Then he said, "I'll tell you. The back door of that No. 2 is the door that comes out into that little close alley between the tavern and the old rattle trap of a brick store. Now you get hold of all the doorkeys you can find, and I'll nip all of Auntie's, and the first dark night we'll go there and try 'em. And mind you, keep a lookout for Injun Joe, because he said he was going to drop into town and spy around once more for a chance to get his revenge. If you see him, you just follow him; and if he don't go to that No. 2, that ain't the place."

That night Tom and Huck were ready for their adventure. They waited near the tavern until after nine, one watching the alley and the other the tavern door. Nobody came into the alley or left it. Tom went home. He knew that Huck would come by and call him and they would slip out and try the keys. But the night remained clear, and Huck went to bed about twelve.

Tuesday was the same. Also Wednesday. But Thursday night was better. Tom slipped out with his aunt's old tin lantern and a large towel to hide it with. The watch began. An hour before midnight the tavern closed and put out its lights. Nobody had entered or left the alley. It was dark and still.

Tom got his lantern, lit it, wrapped it in the towel, and the two adventurers crept toward the tavern. Huck watched while Tom felt his way into the alley. Huck waited and waited. Suddenly there was a flash of light and Tom came rushing by him. "Run!" said he. "Run for your life!"

Once was enough; Huck ran. The boys never stopped till they reached a shed at the lower end of the village. As soon as Tom got his breath back he said, "Huck, it was awful! I tried two of the keys, just as soft as I could; but they seemed to make so much noise, I was so scared. The keys wouldn't turn in the lock, either. I took hold of the knob, and the door opened! It wasn't locked! I hopped in, and Great Caeser's Ghost!"

"What!—what'd you see, Tom?"

"I 'most stepped on Injun Joe's hand!"

"No!"

"Yes! He was lying there, sound asleep on the floor, and his arms spread out."

"What did you do? Did he wake up?"

"No, never budged. Drunk, I reckon. I just grabbed that towel and ran!"

"Tom, did you see that box?"

"Huck, I didn't wait to look around. I didn't see the box, I didn't see the cross. I didn't see anything but a bottle and a tin cup on the floor by Injun Joe; yes, lots more bottles in the room. Don't you

see, now, what's the matter with that ha'nted room?"

"How?"

"Why, it's ha'nted with whiskey! Maybe all the Temperance Taverns have got a ha'nted room, hey, Huck?"

"Well, I reckon maybe that's so. Who'd–a thought such a thing? But say, Tom, now's a mighty good time to get that box, if Injun Joe's drunk."

"It is, that! You try it!"

Huck shuddered.

"Well, no—I reckon not."

"And I reckon not, Huck. Only one bottle alongside of Injun Joe ain't enough. If there'd been three, he'd be drunk enough and I'd do it."

Tom said, "Look here, Huck, let's not try that thing anymore till we know Injun Joe's not in there. It's too scary. Now, if we watch every night, we'll be dead sure to see him go out, and then we'll snatch that box quicker'n lightning."

"Well, I'm agreed. I'll watch the whole night long, and I'll do it every night, too, if you'll do the other part of the job," said Huck.

CHAPTER 15

Huck Saves the Widow

The first thing Tom heard on Friday morning was a piece of good news: Judge Thatcher's family had come back to town the night before. Both Injun Joe and the treasure came second to Becky. They had a good time to playing "hispy" and "gully keeper."

Becky's mother agreed to let them have a picnic the next day. Everyone was thrilled. The invitations were sent out. Tom was so excited, he stayed awake waiting for Huck's call; but he was disappointed. No signal came that night.

The next morning everyone met at Judge Thatcher's. A few young ladies and gentlemen would be in charge. The old steam ferryboat was chartered.

The last thing Mrs. Thatcher said to Becky, was, "You'll not get back till late, child."

"I'll stay with Susy Harper, Mama."

"Very well. And mind and behave yourself and don't be any trouble."

Three miles below town the ferryboat stopped at the mouth of a woody hollow. The crowd went ashore and soon the forest and hills echoed with shouting and laughter. By and by, people came

back to the camp, tired and hungry. After the feast there was a rest. By and by somebody shouted, "Who's ready for the cave?"

Everybody was. Candles in their hands, they ran up the hill. The mouth of the cave was up the hillside—an opening shaped like a letter A. Its massive oak door was open. Inside was a small space, cold, and walled by solid limestone. It was romantic and mysterious to stand there in the gloom and look out over the green valley shining in the sun. Then they started playing again, chasing through the passages in the hill. The candles showed the high walls of rock meeting almost sixty feet overhead. The path was no more than eight or ten feet wide. Every few steps other narrower paths branched off—McDougal's Cave was a vast maze of crooked aisles that ran into one another and out again and led nowhere.

Huck was already upon his watch when the ferryboat's lights went past the wharf. He wondered what boat it was, and why she did not stop at the wharf—and then he forgot her and went back to watching.

He heard a noise. He was all attention in an instant. The alley door closed softly. He sprang to the corner of the brick store. The next moment two men brushed by him, and one seemed to have something under his arm. It must be that box! So they were going to remove the treasure. Why call Tom now? The men would get away with the box and never be found again. No, he would follow them; the dark would hide him well. Huck stepped out and glided along behind the men, allowing them to keep just far enough ahead not to be invisible.

They moved up the river street three blocks, then turned to the left up a cross-street. They went straight ahead, then, until they came to the path that led up to the Cardiff Hill. They passed by the old Welshman's house, halfway up the hill, and still climbed upward. Good, thought Huck, they will bury it in the old quarry. But they never stopped at the quarry. They passed on, up the hill. They plunged into the narrow path between the tall sumac bushes, and were at once hidden in the dark. Huck went closer, for they would never be able to see him. He slowed down, then stopped altogether; listened; no sound; none, save that he seemed to hear the beating of his own heart.

The hooting of an owl came over the hill! But no footsteps. He was about to spring up and run forward, when a man cleared his throat not four feet from him! Huck stood there shaking. He knew where he was. He knew he was within five steps of the stile leading into the Widow Douglas's grounds. Very well, he thought, let them bury it there; it won't

be hard to find.

Now there was a voice—a very low voice—Injun Joe's: "Damn her, she's got company—there's lights, late as it is."

"I can't see any."

This was that stranger's voice—the stranger of the haunted house. A deadly chill went to Huck's heart—this, then, was the "revenge" job! His thought was to run away. Then he remembered that the Widow Douglas had been kind to him more than once, and maybe these men were going to murder her. He wanted to warn her, but he knew he didn't dare—they might come and catch him.

Injun Joe said, "I tell you again, as I've told you before, I don't care for her swag—you may have it. But her husband was rough on me—many times he was rough on me—and mainly he was the justice of the peace that jugged me for a vagrant. He had me horsewhipped!—horsewhipped in front of the jail!—with all the town looking on! horsewhipped!—do you understand? He took advantage of me and died. But I'll take it out on her."

Huck held his breath and stepped back; slowly, carefully, as quietly as he could—

a twig snapped under his foot! His breath stopped and he listened. There was no sound. Then he stepped quickly but carefully along. When he came out of the bushes at the quarry, he felt safe, and so he ran like the wind. Down, he sped, till he reached the Welshman's house. He banged at the door, and soon the heads of the old man and his two big sons looked out of the windows.

"What's the row there? Who's banging? What do you want?"

"Let me in! I'll tell everything."

"Why, who are you?"

"Huckleberry Finn. Quick, let me in!"

"Huckleberry Finn, indeed! It ain't a name to open many doors! But let him in, lads, and let's see what's the trouble."

"Please don't ever tell I told you," were Huck's first words when he got in. "Please don't—I'd be killed, sure—but the widow's been good friends to me sometimes, and I want to tell—I will tell,

if you'll promise you won't ever say it was me."

Three minutes later the old man and his sons, well armed, were up the hill, and just entering the sumac path on tiptoe, their weapons in their hands. Huck went no further. He hid behind a great rock and listened. There was a long silence, and then all of a sudden there was an explosion of guns and a yell.

Huck waited no longer. He ran down the hill as fast as his legs could carry him.

As the new day dawned, Huck came up the hill and rapped gently at the old Welshman's door. A call came from a window, "Who's there?"

Huck's scared voice answered, "Please let me in! It's only Huck Finn!"

The door was quickly unlocked, and he entered. Huck was given a seat and the old man and his tall sons got dressed.

"Well, poor chap, you do look as if you'd had a hard night of it. We knew where to find them, by your description; so we crept along on tiptoe till we got within fifteen feet of them—and just then I found I was going to sneeze. I tried to keep it back, but no use—'twas bound to come, and it did come! I was in the lead and when the sneeze made those scoundrels run, I sung out, 'Fire, boys!' and blazed away. So did the boys. But they were off in a jiffy, those villains, and we after them, down through the woods.

We never touched them. They fired a shot apiece, but their bullets whizzed by. As soon as we lost the sound of their feet, we stopped chasing them, and got the police. They went off to guard the riverbank, and as soon as it was light, the sheriff and a gang will search the woods. My boys will be with them. I wish we had some sort of description of those rascals—'twould help a good deal."

"Oh, yes; I saw them downtown and follered them. One's the old deaf and dumb Spaniard that's been around here, and the other's a mean-looking, ragged—"

"That's enough, lad, we know the men! Off with you, boys, and tell the sheriff!"

The Welshman's sons left at once. Huck sprang up and exclaimed, "Oh, please don't tell anybody it was me!"

"My boy, don't be afraid of me. I'd protect you. This Spaniard is not deaf and dumb—you've let that slip without intending it; you can't cover that up now. You know something about that Spaniard. Now, trust me—tell me what it is."

Huck looked into the old man's eyes a moment, then bent over and whispered, "Tain't a Spaniard—it's Injun Joe!"

The Welshman almost jumped out of his chair. In a moment he said, "It's all plain enough, now. When you talked about notching ears and slitting noses,

I thought it was your imagination, because white men don't take that sort of revenge. But an Injun! That's a different matter."

During breakfast the talk went on. The old man said that before going to bed, he and his sons got a lantern and looked for marks of blood. They found none, but captured a bulky bundle of—

"Of what?"

Huck's eyes were staring wide and his

breath held, waiting for the answer. The Welshman started—stared in return—then replied, "Of burglar's tools. Why, what's the matter with you?"

Huck sank back. The Welshman presently said, "Yes, burglar's tools. What were you expecting we'd found?"

Huck couldn't think of anything to day, so he said, "Sunday School books."

Huck was upset, but the old man laughed. "You ain't well a bit—no wonder you're a little off your balance. But you'll come out of it. Rest and sleep."

Huck felt glad about it all, for now he knew that the bundle was not that bundle, and so his mind was at rest. The treasure must be still in Number Two, the men would be captured and jailed that day, and he and Tom could seize the gold that night without any trouble.

Suddenly there was a knock at the door. The Welshman let in several ladies and gentlemen, among them the Widow Douglas. So the news had spread. The Welshman had to tell the story of the night. The widow's thanks were loud.

"Don't say a word about it, madam. There's someone else you should thank, but he don't allow me to tell his name."

Everybody was early at church. News came that not a sign of the two villains had been found. When the sermon was finished, Judge Thatcher's wife spoke to Mrs. Harper: "Is my Becky going to sleep all day? I expected she would be tired."

"Your Becky?"

"Yes," she said with a startled look. "Didn't she stay with you last night?"

"Why, no."

Mrs. Thatcher turned pale, and just then Aunt Polly, talking briskly with a friend, passed by. Aunt Polly said, "Good morning, Mrs. Thatcher. Good morning, Mrs. Harper. I reckon my Tom stayed at your house last night—one of you. And now he's afraid to come to church."

Mrs. Thatcher shook her head and turned paler than ever.

"He didn't stay with us," said Mrs. Harper. Aunt Polly looked worried.

Children were asked, and young teachers. No one had noticed whether Tom and Becky were on board the ferryboat. One young man finally said that they were probably still in the cave! Mrs. Thatcher fainted, and Aunt Polly started crying.

The alarm was out, and within five minutes the bells were wildly clanging and the whole town was up! Horses were saddled, boats were pushed out, and two hundred men were headed toward the cave.

The search continued. Three dreadful days and nights dragged along.

CHAPTER 16

Lost and Found

Tom and Becky tripped along inside the cave till they came to a place where a little stream of water had formed a laced and ruffled Niagara in gleaming stone. Tom squeezed his small body behind it in order to light it for Becky to see. He found that it hid a sort of steep natural stairway between narrow walls.

Becky and he made a smoke mark to know where they were and started exploring. They walked this way and that, far down into the secret depths of the cave, made another mark, and branched off to find more that they could tell their friends about.

Becky grew apprehensive. "I wonder how long we've been down here, Tom? We better start back."

"Yes, I reckon we better. "

"Can you find the way, Tom? It's all mixed up, to me."

"I reckon I could find it."

"But I hope we won't get lost. It would be so awful!" Becky said as she shuddered.

They went down one path and then another, but none was the right one. At last Becky said, "Tom, Tom, we're lost! We never can get out of this awful place! Oh, why did we ever leave the others!"

She sank to the ground and cried so hard that Tom was afraid. He sat down by her and put his arms around her; she clung to him. Tom begged her to be brave, and she said she could not. He blamed himself; this had a better effect. She said she would try to get up and follow wherever he might lead if only he would not talk like that.

So they moved on again—aimlessly.

At last Becky's limbs were too tired to walk. She sat down. Tom rested with her, and they talked of home, and the friends there and, above all, the light!

They rose up and wandered along, hopeless. For all they knew, they had been there for days and weeks, but that was not true, for their candles were not gone yet. A long time after this Tom said they must go softly and listen for dripping water—they must find a spring. They found one, and Tom said it was time to rest again. Becky burst into tears and said, "Tom! They'll miss us and hunt for us!"

"Yes, they will! Certainly they will!"

"Maybe they're hunting for us now."

"I reckon they are. I hope they are."

The children watched the candle slowly burn down, and slept. After what seemed a long time, both woke up. Tom said it might be Sunday, now—maybe Monday. He tried to get Becky to talk, but she was too upset. Tom said that they must have been missed long ago, and no doubt the search was going on. He would shout and maybe someone would come. He tried it; but in the darkness the distant echoes sounded so horrible that he stopped.

Then Tom said, "Did you hear that?"

Both held their breath and listened. There was a sound like the faintest, far-off shout. Instantly Tom answered it and, leading Becky by the hand, started in its direction. He listened again; again, the sound was heard, and a little nearer.

"It's them!" said Tom. "They're coming! Come along, we're all right now!"

They were overjoyed. They had to go slow since there were many pitfalls and they could not see how deep they were. They came to one and had to stop. Tom lay down. Then he tried to feel for the bottom, but could not. They listened; the distant shoutings slowly faded out! Tom whooped until he was hoarse, but it was of no use. The children groped their way back to the spring. The time dragged on; they slept again, and woke up hungry and miserable. Tom believed it must have been Tuesday by this time.

Now an idea struck him. It would be

better to explore some of these than wait. He took a kite line from his pocket, tied it to a rock, and he and Becky started, Tom in the lead, unwinding the line as they went. After twenty steps it ended in a "jumping-off place." Tom got down on his knees and felt below, and at that moment, not twenty yards away, a human hand, holding a candle, appeared from behind a rock! Tom lifted up a glorious shout, and instantly that hand was followed by the body it belonged to: Injun Joe's! Tom could not move. The next moment, the man vanished. Injun Joe had not recognized Tom's voice. Tom was very scared, but was careful to not tell Becky what he had seen. He told her he had only shouted "for luck."

After another wait at the spring and another long sleep, the children woke up very hungry. Tom believed that it must have been Wednesday or Thursday or even Friday or Saturday, now, and that the search had been stopped. He decided to explore another passage. He was willing to risk Injun Joe and all other terrors. But Becky was very weak. She said she would wait where she was, and die. She told Tom to go with the kite line and explore.

Tom kissed her and made a show of being confident of finding the searchers or an escape from the cave; then he took the kite line in his hand and went down one of the passages on his hands and knees, afraid of what might happen next.

Tuesday passed slowly. The village of St. Petersburg mourned. The lost children had not been found. People prayed for them, but still no good news came from the cave. Most searchers had given up. Mrs. Thatcher was very ill; it was heartbreaking to hear her call her child, and raise her head and listen, then lay it down again with a moan. Aunt Polly was miserable, and her gray hair was almost white.

In the middle of the night the village bells pealed, and in a moment the streets were full of people, who shouted, "They're found! They're found!" The children came in an open carriage, with people cheering around it!

The village was lit up; nobody went to bed again. It was the greatest night the little town had ever seen. During

the first half hour villagers dropped by Judge Thatcher's house, seized the children and kissed them, and went out crying.

Aunt Polly's happiness was complete, and Mrs. Thatcher's nearly so. Hers would be complete as soon as the messenger sent to the cave had told her husband the news. Tom lay upon a sofa surrounded by people and told them about the wonderful adventure.

Tom described how he had left Becky and had gone on an exploring expedition; how he followed two paths as far as his kite line would reach. How he had followed a third, and was about to turn back when he saw a far-off speck that looked like daylight, dropped the line and went toward it, pushed his head and shoulders through a small hole, and saw the Mississippi River rolling by!

And if it had been at night he would not have seen that speck of daylight and would not have explored anymore! He told how he went back for Becky and broke the good news, and she told him not to fret her with such stuff, for she was tired and knew she was going to die. He said how he convinced her; and how she almost died for joy when she actually saw the blue speck of daylight; how he pushed his way out of the hole and then helped her out; how they sat there and cried; how some men came

170

along in a boat and Tom hailed them; how the men didn't believe the wild tale at first, then took them aboard, rowed to a house, gave them supper, made them rest till two or three hours after dark and then brought them home.

Before dawn, Judge Thatcher and the few searchers with him were traced in the cave, and told the great news.

Three days and nights in the cave took time to wear off. Tom and Becky were in bed all Wednesday and Thursday. Tom got about, a little, on Thursday, was downtown Friday, and nearly fine Saturday; but Becky did not leave her room until Sunday.

Tom learned of Huck's sickness and went to see him on Friday, but was not allowed in until Monday. He visited daily after that, but was warned not to say anything about his adventure. The Widow Douglas was there to see that he obeyed. At home, Tom learned of what happened at Cardiff Hill; he also learned that the "ragged man's" body had been found in the river near the ferry landing; he had drowned while trying to escape, perhaps.

About two weeks after Tom's rescue he stopped by judge Thatcher's house to see Becky. The judge and some friends talked to Tom, and some one asked him if he wouldn't like to go to the cave again. Tom said he thought he wouldn't mind it. The judge said, "Well, there are others just like you, Tom. But we have taken care of that. Nobody will get lost in that cave anymore."

"Why?"

"I had its big door shut with iron two weeks ago, and triple locked—and I've got the keys."

Tom turned as white as a sheet. "Oh, Judge, Injun Joe's in the cave!"

CHAPTER 17

Injun Joe is Dead

Very quickly lots of men were on their way to McDougal's Cave. Tom was in the boat with Judge Thatcher.

When the cave door was unlocked, they saw Injun Joe stretched upon the ground, dead, with his face close to the crack of the door. Tom was sad—he knew by his own experience how the man had suffered. But he also felt relieved, because he had been afraid ever since Doctor Robinson's murder.

Injun Joe's knife lay close by, its blade broken in two. The great beam of the door had been chipped and hacked through; the only damage done was to

173

the knife itself.

Injun Joe was buried near the mouth of the cave, and people came there in boats and wagons from all around; they brought their children, and all sorts of food, and said they had as much fun at the funeral as they could have had at the hanging.

"Huck, that money wasn't ever in Number Two!"

"What!" Huck searched his comrade's face keenly. "Tom, have you got on the track of that money again?"

"Huck, it's in the cave!"

"Let's start right off, Tom."

"All right. We want some bread and meat, and a little bag or two, and two or three kite strings, and some of these new lucifer matches. Many's the time I wished I had some when I was in there before."

Just after noon the boys took a small skiff and got under way. They landed.

Tom proudly marched into a thick clump of bushes and said, "Look at it, Huck. It's the snuggest hole in this country. You just keep mum about it."

The boys entered the hole, Tom in the lead. They walked to the far end of the tunnel, then tied together their kite strings and moved on. A few steps brought them to the spring, and Tom felt a shudder go through him. He showed Huck the fragment of candle wick on a lump of clay against the wall, and told how he and Becky had watched the flame fade out.

The boys spoke in whispers and went on, and soon went into Tom's other corridor until they reached the "jumping-off place." The candles showed that it was not really a cliff, but only a steep clay hill.

Tom whispered, "Now I'll show you something, Huck."

He held his candle aloft and said, "Look as far around the corner as you can. Do you see that? There—on the big rock over

yonder—done with candle smoke."

"Tom, it's a cross!"

"Now where's your Number Two? 'Under the cross,' hey? Here's where I saw Injun Joe poke up his candle, Huck!"

Tom went first, cutting rough steps in the clay hill as he went down. Four paths opened out of the small cavern that the great rock stood in. The boys examined three with no result. They found a small hole in the one nearest the rock, with blankets spread in it. But there was no money box. The lads searched, but found nothing.

Tom said, "Look here, Huck. There's footprints and some candle grease on the clay about one side of this rock, but not on the other sides. Now, what's that for? I bet you the money is under the rock. I'm going to dig in the clay."

Tom's had not dug four inches before he struck wood.

"Hey, Huck! You hear that?"

Huck began to dig and scratch now. Some boards were soon uncovered and removed. They had concealed a natural hole under the rock. Tom got into this and held his candle as far under the rock as he could, but said he could not see to the end. He went under, going downward. Tom turned a short curve and exclaimed, "My goodness, Huck, look here!"

It was the treasure box, sure enough, in a snug little cavern, along with an empty powder keg, a couple of guns in leather cases, two or three pairs of old moccasins, a leather belt, and some other rubbish.

"Got it at last!" said Huck. "My, but we're rich, Tom!"

"Huck, I always reckoned we'd got it."

The money was soon in the bags, and the boys took it up to the cross rock.

"Get the guns and things," said Huck.

"No, Huck—leave them there. We'll keep them there all the time, and we'll hold our orgies there, too."

They came out into the clump of bushes, looked out warily, found the coast clear, and were soon lunching. As they went down they got under way. Tom skimmed up the shore, chatting cheerily with Huck, and landed shortly after dark.

"Now, Huck," said Tom, "we'll hide the

money in the loft of the widow's wood-shed, and I'll come up in the morning and we'll count it and then we'll hunt up a place out in the woods where it will be safe."

He disappeared, and presently returned with the wagon, put the two small sacks into it, threw some old rags on top of them, and started off, dragging his cargo behind him. When the boys reached the Welshman's house, they stopped to rest. Just as they were about to move on, the Welshman stepped out and said, "Hallo, who's that?"

"Huck and Tom Sawyer."

"Good! Come along with me, boys. You are keeping everybody waiting. Hurry up. I'll haul the wagon for you. It's not as light as it might be. Got bricks in it? Or old metal?"

"Old metal," said Tom.

Huck found himself pushed, along with Tom, into Mrs. Douglas's drawing room.

Mr. Jones left the wagon near the door and followed.

The place was grandly lit, and everybody in the village was there. Some minutes later the widow's guests were at the supper table. At the proper time Mr. Jones made his little speech, in which he thanked the widow for the honor she was doing himself and his sons, but said that there was another person—

He sprung his secret of Huck's share in the adventure in the finest dramatic manner. The widow heaped so many compliments and so much gratitude upon Huck that he almost forgot the discomfort of his new clothes in the discomfort of being a target for everybody's gaze and praise.

The widow said she meant to give Huck a home under her roof and have him educated. Tom's chance had come. He said, "Huck don't need it. Huck's rich.

Huck's got money. Maybe you don't believe it, but he's got lots of it. Oh, you needn't smile—I reckon I can show you."

Tom ran out of doors. The company looked at one another.

"What ails Tom?" asked Aunt Polly. "There ain't ever making that boy out."

Tom entered, struggling with the weight of his sacks. Tom poured the mass of yellow coins upon the table and said, "There—what did I tell you? Half of it's Huck's and half of it's mine!"

CHAPTER 18

Tom and Huck Become Rich

The heap of gold coins took everyone's breath away. They all wanted to know what was going on. Tom told the whole story.

The money was counted. It was twelve thousand dollars.

Tom and Huck's windfall made a mighty stir in the poor little village of St. Petersburg. They were admired and stared at. The village paper published their stories.

The Widow Douglas put Huck's money out at six percent. Judge Thatcher did the same with Tom's, at Aunt Polly's request. Each lad had an income.

Judge Thatcher hoped to see Tom a
great lawyer or a great soldier someday. He said he meant to see that Tom
was admitted to the National Military
Academy and afterward trained in the
best law school in the country.

Huck Finn's wealth and Widow
Douglas's protection introduced him
into society. The widow's servants
kept him clean and neat. He had to

eat with a knife and a fork; he had to use a napkin, cup, and plate; he had to learn his books; he had to go to church; he had to talk properly.

He bravely bore his miseries three weeks, and then one day went missing. The widow hunted for him everywhere. The public searched high and low; they dragged the river for his body. Then Tom went poking among

some old empty hogsheads behind the abandoned slaughterhouse, and in one of them he found him. Huck had slept there—unkempt, uncombed, and clad in the same old rags he'd had before, when he was free and happy. Tom urged him to go home.

Huck said, "Don't talk about it, Tom. I've tried it, and it don't work; it ain't for me. The widder's good to me, and friendly, but I can't stand them ways. She makes me get up at the same time every morning; she makes me wash; she won't let me sleep in the woodshed; I got to go to church and sweat, and sweat! I got to wear shoes all Sunday. The widder eats by a bell; she goes to bed by a bell; she gits up by a bell—everything's so awful reg'lar, a body can't stand it."

"Huck, being rich ain't going to keep me back from turning robber. We can't let you into the gang if you ain't respectable, you know."

"Can't let me in, Tom? Didn't you let me go for a pirate?"

"Yes, but that's different. A robber is more high-toned than what a pirate is. In most countries they're awful high up in the nobility—dukes and such."

"Now, Tom, hain't you always ben friendly to me? You wouldn't shet me out, would you?"

"Huck, I wouldn't want to, but what would people say?"

Huck was silent for some time. Finally he said, "Well, I'll go back to the widder for a month and tackle it if you'll let me b'long to the gang, Tom."

"All right, Huck, it's a whiz! Come along, old chap. I'll ask the widow to let up on you a little."

"Now, that's something like! Why, it's a million times bullier than pirating. I'll stick to the widder till I rot, Tom; and if I git to be a reg'lar ripper of a

robber, and everybody talking 'bout it,
I reckon she'll be proud she snaked
me in out of the wet."

About the Author

Samuel Clemens, also known as Mark Twain, was born in Florida, Missouri, on November 30, 1835, to a Tennessee country merchant, John Marshall Clemens. He was an American humorist, satirist, lecturer, and writer.

Twain is most noted for his novels. *The Adventures of Tom Sawyer* is considered a "Great American Novel." *The Adventures of Tom Sawyer* and *Huckleberry Finn* derive from Twain's childhood experiences.

He wrote these books to entertain boys and girls and hoped that the books would help them to recall their own childhood.

Twain died in 1910. *The Adventures of Tom Sawyer* was both an American classic and a best-seller. It is arguably the work for which Twain is best known today.

Treasury of Illustrated Classics™